Groundwood Books / House of Anansi Press
110 Spadina Avenue, Suite 801, Toronto, Ontario M5V 2K4
or c/o Publishers Group West
1700 Fourth Street, Berkeley, CA 94710

We acknowledge for their financial support of our publishing
program the Canada Council for the Arts, the Ontario Arts Council
and the Government of Canada.

Canada Council   Conseil des Arts
for the Arts   du Canada

ONTARIO ARTS COUNCIL
CONSEIL DES ARTS DE L'ONTARIO
an Ontario government agency
un organisme du gouvernement de l'Ontario

With the participation of the Government of Canada | Canadä
Avec la participation du gouvernement du Canada

Library and Archives Canada Cataloguing in Publication
Vande Griek, Susan, author
Go Home Bay / written by Susan Vande Griek ; illustrated by
Pascal Milelli.
Issued in print and electronic formats.
ISBN 978-1-55498-701-6 (bound).—ISBN 978-1-55498-702-3 (pdf)
1. Thomson, Tom, 1877-1917—Juvenile fiction. I. Milelli,
Pascal, illustrator II. Title.
PS8593.A53855G64 2016   jC813'.54   C2015-903609-7
C2015-903610-0

The color illustrations were done in oil on canvas, and the vignette
sketches in pencil.
Design by Michael Solomon
Printed and bound in Malaysia

For Justin and Julia
who led me to Ross King's *Defiant Spirits*
which led me to a story— SVG

To Jeffrey Ryan — PM

Go Home Bay

Susan Vande Griek

PICTURES BY

Pascal Milelli

GROUNDWOOD BOOKS

HOUSE OF ANANSI PRESS

TORONTO   BERKELEY

On West Wind Island,
at Go Home Bay,
I'm swimming — brrr —
picnicking,
rowing,
reading
through the long and away
June, July days.

Gentle the west wind blows.

And then one afternoon
comes
a Chestnut canoe,
painted gray-blue,
packed full of
fishing gear,
camping gear,
painting gear
and steered by a man,
paddle in hand.

He steps out on our dock —
tall.
Over one eye
his dark hair falls,
and my father says,
"Helen, meet Mr. Thomson.
He's come to stay."

I shake his hand,
tanned and strong,
paint-stained,
as he says, "Hello.
Just call me Tom."

His khaki pants and woodsman shirt
smell of campfires
and all outdoors.

While he and my father
have a lively chat
about paintings and artists
and a lake named Canoe,
about fishing and camping
and paddling trips,
Tom builds a campfire
and sets up a pot,
into which he tosses some of this,
some of that.

It boils and bubbles.
I bring more wood.
And after it cooks,
he shares with us
his tasty supper of
mulligatawny stew.

Fresh the west wind blows.

In the island morning
I wake and watch
as out on the bay
Tom the fisherman goes.
He sits quiet and still,
casting out,
reeling in.

With a string of fish,
he paddles back
and then fries up
a lunchtime snack.

I follow behind
in the afternoon breeze,
as Tom the painter hikes
the island's edge
to a spot where he stops
and from his painter's box
takes palette and brush,
oils and board
and sketches there,
the bay's choppy water
slapping rocky shores.

I look out from the dock
at the sun-end of day,
as Tom the canoeist
paddles out and about,
dip, dribble, glide,
on a now so-calm bay.
He's at home with the call of the loon,
alone with the rose-blue sky.

Light the west wind blows.

And one July day
Tom says to me,
"Let's paint the wildflowers
by the cottage door."

He gives me oils and brush
and palette knife,
shows me how to petal them,
color them, shape them,
make them bloom on a little board.

He takes me down
onto the dock.
Blobs of paint
we spread and scrape
to sketch our rowboat
and his canoe.

And in the brilliant light
of that sunshine day,
he says,
"Let's paint
the houseboat, too,
in the roses and greens,
the pinks and blues,
all the colors of
Go Home Bay."

Wild the west wind blows.

"Quick!" Tom calls.
"Let's paint a pine."

And down by the shore,
clothes flapping, we go.
Dark clouds cluster,
the air blusters and puffs.

Tom points and shouts,
"See how the branches
sway and bend."
So we paint them out over water,
west wind sent,
trees that are forever
west wind bent.

We slap down our colors,
green branches,
gray trunk,
faster, faster,
rush to paint water,
white-capped,
riled up.

Until thunder mumbles
and raindrops tumble
and we must gather
our paints, our boards,
then hurry to huddle
and watch from the cottage door.

Cool the west wind blows.

Tom keeps me up
in the summer dark
to go out at night
to the blue-black sky,
paint moonlight on water,
moon over branches,
bright, up high.
And he guides my hand.
He guides my eye.

The sketches stack up.
My father smiles
and nods
and examines each one,
while Tom and I,
though mostly Tom,
paint
on and on,
throughout July.

Away the west wind blows.

Summer is going,
and so is Tom.
One day
he paddles off
in the gray-blue canoe,
packed full
of fishing gear,
camping gear,
painting gear.

We wave goodbye,
my father and I,
while I hold tight
to a Go Home Bay,
all pink and bright,
to remember a time,
a certain July,
when Tom Thomson
came by and
taught me to paint.

Tom Thomson 1877-1917

Tom Thomson was one of Canada's wonderful painters of nature. During his short life he painted, again and again, the trees, hills, lakes and rocky shores of northern Ontario. His use of rich color and thick paint to express his enthusiasm for the natural world set him apart from many other artists.

Thomson was born in Ontario in 1877 and grew up on a farm with many brothers and sisters. He enjoyed music, drawing and reading as well as outdoor activities such as fishing, farm chores and studying nature. As an adult he worked as a graphic designer in Toronto, where he also used a small shack as an artist's studio.

But Tom often escaped to the outdoors, especially to Ontario's Algonquin Park and Canoe Lake, where he loved painting, fishing, canoeing and camping for months at a time. Tom sometimes asked his artist friends to join him there. These other painters would later form The Group of Seven and become famous for their landscape paintings.

Dr. James MacCallum, a Toronto ophthalmologist at the time, liked Thomson's paintings as well as those of these other artists. He encouraged, supported and spent time with many of them, and he bought many of Tom's paintings.

During the summer of 1914, Dr. MacCallum invited Tom to stay and paint at his cottage on Georgian Bay. While he was there, Thomson gave some art lessons to the doctor's ten-year-old daughter, Helen. When he left the MacCallums' cottage, Tom gave Helen an oil sketch of the houseboat, which was later named "Boathouse, Go Home Bay." On the back of it she wrote, "Given to me by Tom Thomson the summer he taught me to paint."

Helen kept the small painting all her life, leaving it to a relative when she died. Only years later did another family member recognize that it was a work by Tom Thomson, by then considered one of Canada's best-known artists.

"Boathouse, Go Home Bay," the painting, is still privately owned. However, many of Tom Thomson's other paintings can be seen at the Art Gallery of Ontario in Toronto, the National Gallery of Canada in Ottawa and at the McMichael Canadian Art Collection in Kleinburg, Ontario.

Go Home Bay, the story, with imagined scenes and dialogue, is loosely based on the summer events of 1914.

— Susan Vande Griek

FOR FURTHER INFORMATION

Books

The Group of Seven and Tom Thomson: An Introduction by Anne Newlands, Firefly Books, 2008 (for young readers)

Tom Thomson: An Introduction to His Life and Art by David P. Silcox, Firefly Books, 2002

A Treasury of Tom Thomson by Joan Murray, Douglas & McIntyre, 2012

DVDs

The Group of Seven for the Young at Art, McMichael Canadian Art Collection, 2007

West Wind: The Vision of Tom Thomson by Peter Raymont and Michèle Hozer, White Pine Pictures, 2012

Website

http://tomthomsonart.ca